STO

MISTLETOE:
Fact and Folklore

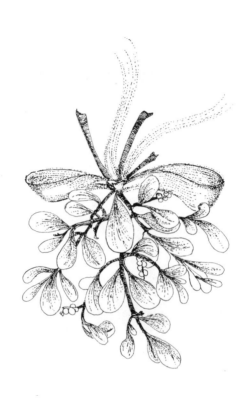

MISTLETOE:
Fact and Folklore

Gray Johnson Poole

Illustrated by Melissa Meredith

DODD, MEAD & COMPANY • NEW YORK

Library of Congress Cataloging in Publication Data

Poole, Gray Johnson.
    Mistletoe, fact and folklore.
    Includes index.
    1.   Mistletoe—Juvenile literature.   2.   Mistletoe
(in religion, folk-lore, etc.)—Juvenile literature.
I.   Title.
QK495.L87P66   583'.94   75-38368
ISBN 0-396-07310-7

THIS BOOK IS FOR
SUE ALEXANDER
a.k.a. SIMONE LEGREE

Acknowledgments

Book prefaces and acknowledgments often, with reason and in sincerity, cite someone "without whom this book could not have been written."

For me, in this instance, that person is Dr. Frank G. Hawksworth, plant pathologist, United States Department of Agriculture, Forest Service. Throughout my research for and writing of this book, Dr. Hawksworth gave me his enthusiastic cooperation and provided me with valuable written materials and photographs. His offer to read the manuscript was gladly accepted. He has my deep gratitude on all counts.

I am also indebted to Dr. Donald M. Knutson, plant pathologist, United States Department of Agriculture, Forest Service, for his cooperation and a reading of the manuscript.

As often before on completion of a book, I find myself in debt to many people. For quite special reasons, I express my thanks for assistance to Suzanne Zajac, Roswell Park Memorial Institute, Department of Health, State of New York; Dr. Julian C. Crane, Professor of Pomology, University of California, Davis; the late Dr. Oliver A. Leonard, botanist, University of California, Davis; R. W. Elliott & Sons, A. H. Cole; Bob Graham, Inc., Vickie Andrews, Bud Hershfeld, Dick Andrews; Dennis-Landman, publishers, J. Noel Dennis; David L. Graham, University Relations, University of Oklahoma; Dr. Frank C. Craighead, the Environmental Research Institute (Wyoming) and the State University of New York.

To many others too numerous to list I am also most grateful.

G. J. P.
Los Angeles, California

Contents

1

❧❧❧❧❧

The Mistletoes

Mistletoe is a traditional Christmas decoration in many lands. Throughout the United States, it is displayed in small shops and huge department stores, in public buildings and business offices. In American homes, mistletoe hangs from door lintels and is bunched on fireplace mantels.

You undoubtedly can identify holiday sprays of green leaves with clusters of whitish berries as mistletoe. But do you know there are many other kinds?

In fact, the botanical family of mistletoes consists of about 65 related groups, or genera, with more than 1,300 species, or separate forms.

Mistletoes are unusual plants and their history is fascinating. All are destructive to other plants. Some are pretty; others, ugly.

Livestock and wildlife, including birds, safely feed on mistletoes. For some reason, not known, most kinds of mistletoe berries poison human beings. But medicine made from properly treated

Mistletoe is a traditional Christmas decoration in many lands.

11

juice of the berries cured sick people in ages past. And, as a result of modern experiments and research, medicine from mistletoe may become a major lifesaver of the future.

Mistletoes are parasite plants, pests that live on other plants. The parasites take what they need to survive. Some mistletoe depends totally on the plant it grows on for food, moisture, and necessary nutrients. Other mistletoe requires only water and

European mistletoe in cross section of apple wood

12

minerals from the plant, called a host.

The host, whether a tree, bush or shrub, is always damaged and sometimes killed by the parasite mistletoe.

Most mistletoes are aerial. They grow on trunks, limbs, branches, the upper parts of hosts. A very few mistletoes are terrestrial. They grow in soil. Like aerial mistletoes, the terrestrial ones are parasites and live off other plants. The earth-growing mistletoes are bushes, shrubs or very small trees of the tropics. They reach out with their roots and steal nourishment from roots of nearby host plants.

Perhaps millions of years ago many species of mistletoe had roots in the ground. If so, most of those types gradually lost what botanists call the "terrestrial root mode." The plants slowly, by evolution, became parasites with roots in bark and wood above the ground.

A mistletoe plant sprouts from a seed. The seed sticks to the bark of a branch, a limb, or the trunk of a host. Viscin, a gummy substance around the seed, is similar to glue or mucilage. On the host, the viscin hardens like a cement of which sidewalks and building blocks are made.

When in place the seed sends out a holdfast from which a rootlet, or haustorium, develops. Depending on the species of mistletoe, its root system spreads a short distance, or long, under the bark or in the wood of the host. Time of development also depends on species.

Flowers bloom on stems; some have leaves, some are leafless. There are genera of mistletoe with male and female flowers on separate plants. Dioecious is the word for plants with flowers of individual sex. Birds, insects, and wind variously transfer male pollen from one plant to the female flower on another.

Other genera of mistletoe have male and female parts in a single flower. The male pollen drops into the female ovary

13

where the seed develops. Selfing is what botanists call that kind of pollination. It is self-pollination.

Pollinated flowers produce fruit, the mistletoe berry. It contains the seed surrounded by viscin.

Some trees will not play host to mistletoe. The beefwood, or she-oak of Australia, is typical of trees that protect themselves from mistletoe.

When a holdfast develops from a seed on a beefwood tree, gum oozes out of the bark and prevents growth of a rootlet, the haustorium. The tree exudes or sweats gum the way the human body gives off perspiration.

Trees on other continents repel mistletoe the same way. As long ago as 1917, scientific observers reported the rejection of mistletoe seeds by yew trees in England.

One of the strange things about mistletoes is the growth of one on another. A seed of a species may land on a bushy mass or clump of mistletoe already rooted in a host. Moisture, food, and minerals from the host are taken by the established mistletoe and shared by it with the second.

The parasite-mistletoe on a mistletoe-parasite is a little like piggyback trucks loaded with automobiles. The automobiles hitch rides on their own kind.

Hosts to mistletoe sometimes vary even within a small area. Mistletoe may infect a certain kind of host at one location but not the same kind growing no more than five miles away.

Mistletoes grow in all parts of the world but arctic regions. In various lands the parasites damage park trees; infect timber trees; reduce crops of coffee, rubber, nuts, mangos, avocados, apples, cherries, citrus fruits and pears.

One species of mistletoe in India is found on 330 different host trees.

The best-known mistletoes in the United States are the leafless dwarf mistletoe, genus *Arceuthobium*, and two species with leaves: *Viscum album* (*V. album*) and *Phoradendron flavescens* (*P. flavescens*).

V. album, the common European leafy mistletoe, crossed the Atlantic Ocean as an undiscovered stowaway inside a host plant. The foreign parasite migrated from the East Coast to northern California.

P. flavescens is native to the United States, and about 200 species of its genus *Phoradendron* grow in North and South America.

2

❧❧❧❧❧

Berries for the Birds

Berries of leafy mistletoes are a favorite food of many kinds of birds throughout the world.

The berry-eating birds unfortunately sow seeds of the kinds of mistletoes they eat. Undigested seeds in bird droppings are deposited on limbs or branches of the hosts. Whole seeds are sometimes left on bark by birds cleaning the mistletoe's sticky berries from their bills. Seeds may sprout on small trees or tall, on low shrubbery or high.

Mango and other tropical trees are deformed by mistletoe planted by small, bright-colored birds, the flowerpeckers. They are native to Taiwan, the Philippines, Australia, and parts of India. One flowerpecker species in Australia is called the mistletoe bird.

Flowerpeckers are named for their habit of pecking into blossoms for nectar and for insect food. But the tiny birds, less than four inches long, also enjoy fruits, especially the berries of

The mistle thrush prefers mistletoe berries but will eat other types of berries as well.

Birds were captured by painting twigs with birdlime, a major ingredient of which is the viscin of certain mistletoe seeds.

tropical mistletoes.

Flowerpeckers not only spread mistletoe seeds, they help to pollinate the parasite. The birds carry pollen from a male flower on one plant to a female flower on another.

The spreading of mistletoe in Europe is aided by a bird related to the robin. Known as the mistle thrush, the missel thrush, or mistletoe thrush, the bird winters in Africa. It migrates north from January to March, and feeds en route chiefly on mistletoe berries.

Migration of the mistle thrush is occasionally delayed by severe storms and intense cold spells in Europe. The birds do not leave Africa until weather to the north is fair. When the birds fail to arrive in time to plant seeds from berries, the European mistletoe crop is reduced.

For centuries some kinds of birds were indirectly victims of mistletoe. The viscin of certain mistletoe seeds was one ingredient used to produce birdlime. That glue-like substance was painted on twigs to capture the birds, primarily for food. When they landed on the birdlime, their tiny claws stuck tight.

Even today, the gluey birdlime is used, in some parts of the world, to trap prized songbirds. They are collected, caged, and sold as household pets.

Countless other wild birds depend on various species of mistletoe for food. Seeds of mistletoe berries keep those birds alive and free.

You do not dare to find out whether you like the taste of mistletoe berries or their seeds. They could poison you. It is not safe to put the sticky berries in your mouth.

And, please, do not let a younger sister or younger brother eat even one mistletoe berry.

As food, the mistletoes are not for human beings. Livestock and wild animals eat whole branches of the parasite. The berries are for the birds.

3

❦❦❦❦❦

Food for Animals

Mistletoes are major pests in Australia but provide food for livestock. Camels, imported as work animals to carry heavy loads, munch on mistletoe. Cattle and sheep also are nourished by some kinds of mistletoe growing on the island continent.

The range animals crop mistletoe from shrubs or from low tree limbs. Camels, with their advantage of height, yank mistletoe from upper branches.

Mistletoe species as food for woodland and domestic animals vary with continents and with regions of a country. Wild animals chiefly feed on leafy mistletoes but some graze on the leafless dwarf mistletoes. Leafy mistletoes are forage for livestock and barnyard animals.

In forests of Turkey, local cattle raisers do more damage to trees than the mistletoe growing on them. Turkish stockmen, without a thought for tree conservation, recklessly collect mistletoe for their herds. Branches and limbs are hacked off the trees.

Mistletoe is often broken from trees by storms and falls to the ground where it is eaten by animals.

Axes mutilate even tree trunks if chunks of mistletoe stick out of the bark.

Leafy mistletoe in Europe is eaten by woodland animals and is harvested for livestock. The parasite is a staple feed for hogs and cattle in some parts of the United States. In other sections, it is substitute fodder especially in dry seasons or unusually cold ones. At times of drought, leafy mistletoe is cut for fodder from mesquite, a spiny tree or shrub that is wild and abundant in Texas. Cattle there are also fed the mesquite's sugary pods, similar in shape to those of peas and beans.

Ranchers, farmers, and scientific experts think perhaps some mistletoe species are bad for pregnant animals. Eating the plants may cause cows to have stillborn calves, and ewes to give birth to stillborn kids.

Deer graze on leafy mistletoes, a fact known long ago to Indians of California. Hunters of tribes gathered the parasite and heaped it in a clearing of the forest. Deer, attracted to the pile of mistletoe, were perfect targets for hunters hiding close-by.

Dependence of elk on dwarf mistletoe as winter forage came as a surprise to scientists studying the animals.

The elk in the Old Faithful area of Yellowstone Park were in a study project of Dr. Frank C. Craighead, Jr., and Dr. John J. Craighead. The two biologists, twin brothers, began their elk study in 1965.

Some of the elk were tracked down by biotelemetry, a system for transmitting and receiving physical facts about living things. For animal studies, transmitters are attached to subjects, and recorded information is relayed to receiving instruments at an information center.

For the Craigheads' study, darts, similar to hypodermic needles, shot a muscle-relaxing drug into the elk subjects. The

Dependence of elk on dwarf mistletoe as winter forage came as a surprise to scientists.

harmless drug kept each elk docile just long enough for a collar to be fastened around its neck.

Telemetering instruments were attached to the collars. Various miniature transistors provided facts about individual and group behavior of the elk. Their movements and range within Yellowstone Park were charted at the Craigheads' field laboratory.

23

Records were kept of activities in various seasons of the year. Food habits of elk in spring, summer, fall, and winter were studied.

Transmitters and other tracking methods indicated an unusual midwinter food selection. The elk were browsing in a forest stand of lodgepole pines. The Craigheads did not understand why because, as they wrote in their project report, "Lodgepole pine forage is not highly palatable to elk."

Guided by the miniature radio collars on the elk, the experts watched the animals feed. They were not eating branches of the lodgepole pine trees but were "feeding almost entirely on dwarf mistletoe" that grows profusely on the pines.

The study had uncovered a fact not previously known. In winter, dwarf mistletoe is a staple diet of elk in the Old Faithful area.

Elk thrive on the same parasite that, in time, kills the lodgepole pines.

4

Little but Lethal

Dwarf mistletoe seeds are wonders of nature. They shoot through the air like launched missiles.

The velocity of the seeds has been calculated through the use of high-speed photography. Scientific studies prove the first burst of speed of the tiny kernels is equal to sixty miles an hour.

Deadly dwarf mistletoe plants are produced by the miniature projectiles. The parasites annually cause millions of dollars of damage to cone-bearing trees in certain western areas of the United States.

Two things keep dwarf mistletoe from being a worse pest than it is: One is the short distance a seed travels from parent parasite to new host. The other is the slow development of roots, flowers, and fruit.

There are no leaves, as usually recognized. Instead, the dwarf mistletoe's stem has thin formations called scales, or bud scales or leaf scales.

The fast-moving seeds, on an average, travel no more than ten to fifteen feet. With a tail wind, seeds may go a bit farther.

The speeding seeds are too small to be seen in action. If you

Dwarf mistletoe on pine
(female plant on left, male plant on right)

look up at an infected tree, you can see neither the launch of a tiny seed from its leafless plant nor the landing on target. Even close at hand, seeds of dwarf mistletoe can best be examined through a magnifying glass.

The seed's holdfast clings to the host's twig, and the rootlet, or haustorium, enters the wood. Roots take their own good time about developing inside the host. They may mature in two years, or in three, four, or five.

When roots are mature, shoots break through the bark. Flowers take another couple of years to develop. A single seed is produced in each fruit about a year later.

Dwarf mistletoe is one of the genera with flowers of separate sexes. The anther, or pollen sac, of the male flower is yellow. Pollination is by various insects, depending on the dwarf mistletoe species, the host, and the region.

Flowers and the berry-fruits are small and homely. The inconspicuous flowers are the same colors as their shoots. The berries, in somewhat similar shades, are about the size of grains of wheat.

Shoots, flowers, and berries can be red, orange, purple, green, yellow, or black. That might indicate dwarf mistletoe clumps are colorful. They are not. Their colors do not show because all parts of the parasite are so small. The effect of the entire growing plant is dull and drab. Scientists identify the colors by studies with magnifying glasses and through microscopes.

When a berry is nearly ripe, the viscin around the seed soaks up moisture from the host. Water pressure builds up inside the berry and finally forces it from the stem. At that moment, the single seed is shot out of the berry. Many seeds launched from ripe dwarf mistletoe fruits drop to the ground. Others land on hosts.

Dwarf mistletoes infect trees and shrubbery throughout the world. But nowhere are the dwarf species more damaging than in the American Southwest and Northwest. The parasites attack conifer forests in Arizona, California, New Mexico, Oregon, and Washington. No other pest of the forests kills more cone-bearing trees, including pines, hemlock, larch, spruce, true fir, and Douglas fir.

Dependent on its host for all life support, dwarf mistletoe steals its food, moisture, nutrients, vitamins, and minerals. A young host-tree, still growing, suffers from the loss of those vital substances.

Unfortunately there are more flowers and berries of dwarf mistletoe on young wood than on old timber. The younger the host, the faster the parasite develops and spreads—and the more quickly the tree is weakened and killed.

Whatever the age of an infected tree, its growth is retarded. The crown, or top of the tree, becomes bare; needles lose their color and drop from branches. The dwarf mistletoe very often makes its host ugly by causing witches'-broom on exposed, bare sections of the host.

Witches'-broom is a bushy growth that disfigures trees and shrubs infected by various attackers. Made up of thin branches, witches'-broom forms in clumps at the crown and on upper limbs stripped of either leaves or needles.

A tree already injured by dwarf mistletoe is an easy victim for pests like insects or fungi, and for viruses and other diseases. All can cause witches'-broom. They also affect the quality of wood, making it unsuitable for use as lumber.

Three billion board feet of lumber are lost every year as a result of dwarf mistletoe infection of conifers.

Dr. Frank G. Hawksworth, leading authority on dwarf mistletoe, suggests a dramatic comparison for three billion board feet: Imagine a board one-inch thick by twelve-inches wide and 625,000 miles in length. That is the distance to the moon and back, plus five times around the earth's equator.

Experts constantly seek ways to rid conifer forests of the mistletoe. Individual infected trees can be removed; or infected branches cut off. A drastic method sometimes used is clear-

Witches'-broom, a bushy growth of weird shape, disfigures the tree.

28

cutting. That is the logging term for chopping down an entire stand of trees. The cleared area is then planted with healthy seedlings.

Studies of other controls of dwarf mistletoe are experimental. Some depend on chemical sprays and chemical injections; others on research with insects and organisms destructive to the parasite.

Birds may be occasional carriers of dwarf mistletoe seeds over long distance. But the sticky seeds probably are on the feathers, not in bird droppings.

Short-range sowing of seeds by birds could happen during nest building in conifer trees. Certain birds build with lichens and mosses from the forest floor. And those plants sometimes contain active, living dwarf mistletoe seeds that did not land on hosts.

5

꽃꽃꽃

Handsome but Harmful

Leafy mistletoes, the holiday decoration species, are really pretty. Their leaves are deep green and their berries, soft white, like pearls. Tiny sprigs of the mistletoes, packaged in clear plastic bags, are stocked by supermarkets. Larger sprays are sold by florists and by Christmas tree dealers.

The seasonal popularity of leafy mistletoes does not mean they are admired by everybody. They are not.

Leafy mistletoes are year-round pests of crop, shade, and ornamental trees. Although only partial parasites, leafy mistletoes present problems to certain people: growers of fruit orchards and nut groves, city and county horticulturists, park superintendents and home owners.

Unlike dwarf mistletoes, leafy mistletoes are fast growing. Germination begins as soon as a seed's holdfast forms. A plant with developed roots is established in about a year. Stems are green like the fleshy leaves. Flowers are dioecious and mostly small. Pollination is by insects. The white glossy berries are the fruits.

The American *P. flavescens* and the European *V. album* look

so much alike they are often mistaken for each other, or thought to be the same kind. Actually the American species has wider leaves and smaller berries than the European.

Leafy mistletoes live long and grow old with the trees they infect. Hosts weaken slowly because the parasites manufacture their own food, taking just water and minerals from their hosts.

The food-making process of leafy mistletoes depends on chlorophyll, the coloring substance in all green plants. Chlorophyll produces carbohydrates, including sugar and starches, by photosynthesis. That is the system in nature by which sunlight is used as the source of energy.

Hosts, giving up moisture and nutrients to leafy mistletoes, dry out and lose strength. Brittle branches and even large limbs may break off when lashed by windstorms. The attached parasites go down with the tree sections, and, like them, wither and die on the ground.

Trees weakened by leafy mistletoes, like those infected by dwarf mistletoes, are exposed to damage from insects, fungi, and various diseases. Those destructive attackers and even a drought of long duration can kill an infected tree. The parasite, deprived of essentials for life, also dies.

If a pest or disease first attacks a leafy mistletoe, it passes the infection to the host. Again both host and parasite suffer.

Some leafy mistletoes are parasitic to a single kind of tree. A species in France infects only white fir. The pest annually accounts for the loss of sixty to eighty million board feet of lumber from white-fir forests.

One American mistletoe grows only on juniper. That particular species is one of the few *Phoradendron* without green leaves. It has leaf scales like those of all dwarf mistletoes.

American mistletoe growing on a branch

33

The European mistletoe, *V. album*, is a newcomer to the United States where it was first identified in 1920. The plant was established on a tree growing near Sebastopol, Sonoma County, California. A specimen of the mistletoe, attached to a branch of its host, was sent to the herbarium of the California Academy of Sciences, San Francisco.

Nearly a decade later a second observer in Sonoma County identified another plant of *V. album* and sent it to the Dudley Herbarium at Stanford University.

European leafy mistletoe steadily spread through the countryside around Sebastopol. But the parasite was not reported by botanists or by owners of infected trees. Apparently those who saw *V. album* mistook it for *P. flavescens* already growing in the region.

Not until 1966 was *V. album* recognized as a parasite established in a 16-square-mile area within the boundary of Sebastopol and adjacent to it. Surveys taken in 1971 showed *V. album* to be growing on 310 host plants of twenty-one tree species. The parasite was on trees in orchards and gardens, along fence rows and sidewalk curbs.

Methods for control of leafy mistletoes in the United States range from mild to severe. Experiments are done with pruning, poisoning, and burning plants. Forest trees, seriously infected, are individually chopped down.

Pruning leafy mistletoe from dormant trees before seeds form is effective in some cases. The use of pruning techniques is recommended for trees in apple orchards, for shade trees on lawns, and for ornamentals in gardens. Annual pruning helps to keep the trees in pleasing shapes with limbs well-balanced.

Every cut has to be sealed. The sealer protects the exterior bark and the interior wood against invasion by insects and bacteria.

34

After the mistletoe is cut away, the trunk or big limb is wrapped with black polyethylene, tied tight to the bark.

It is not possible to prune the trunk or a major limb of an infected tree. The mistletoe has to be cut off straight along the bark. That method keeps seeds from developing but does not reduce growth of roots already inside the wood.

A treatment to kill the root system is quite simple. After the mistletoe is cut away, the trunk or big limb is wrapped with black polyethylene. It is tied tight to the bark with flexible tape

35

or heavy cord. The material has to extend beyond the cut section in order to keep the leafy mistletoe roots in the dark.

Without sunlight as the energy source for production of their food, the roots will die, usually within a year.

Chemical controls for leafy mistletoes are under study and in use. During dormant periods, a chemical solution is a treatment for trees in California walnut orchards where leafy mistletoes thrive. The liquid is injected into the bark or is applied externally, by brush or by spray.

Some plant pathologists disapprove of chemical controls in whatever form.

Warnings of those experts are: Injections cause trees to lose their leaves and might kill the trees faster than mistletoe. There is also danger of absorption of a chemical by any tree painted with it. A drift from windblown spray is a hazard to nearby trees, bushes, or shrubs that are healthy and not infected by mistletoe.

The most drastic plan for mistletoe control is occasionally proposed in American cities. Some of those responsible for maintenance of urban parks, parkways, and plantings along sidewalk curbs favor complete removal of infected trees. Chopping trees down costs less than annual pruning or other regular treatment.

The removal plan is not welcomed by everybody. Many city dwellers want to have the pretty parasites available for easy picking at holiday time.

Harvesting mistletoe from forest trees is a December project for Boy Scouts in regions where the parasite grows. As locale and climate vary, so do the operational plans and procedures of individual troops.

The general schedule of Boy Scout Troop 130, Santa Monica, California, can be an example: For several years the troop chose a mid-December Saturday for picking and packaging the supply for its Annual Mistletoe Sale.

Arangements were made for members of the cub pack and troop by Mary Cooley and her husband, Scoutmaster Richard Cooley. With them, the Scouts and their parents drove to Crystal Lake in mountains northeast of Los Angeles.

There was a ten dollar charge for a one-day permit to gather mistletoe at the Crystal Lake Recreation Area. The Forest Ranger Station there was Scout headquarters for that particular Saturday.

Fathers of the Scouts climbed oak trees and clipped off mistletoe with cutters borrowed from a tree service company. On an informal assembly line, the Scouts and their mothers sorted mistletoe and packaged it in clear plastic bags.

In an average year, one hundred pounds of mistletoe were picked. Packages, numbering from 600 to 800, depending on the year's poundage, were priced at fifty cents. Profits were spent for badges and for the Scout troop's outings to amusement attractions.

The mistletoe was sold door-to-door, or to passersby on city streets. The three members of Troop 130 who sold the largest number of packages were given as prizes money, a medal, and a photograph of the whole group taken at the Forest Ranger Station on the day of the mistletoe picking.

Some Boy Scouts are among the children who annually help adults gather mistletoe in the Texas counties Mills and Williamson. Harvesting, from about November 20 to December 20, is a community effort. Business people, homemakers, artists, writers, and other professionals, and the youngsters, all are paid by the pound for mistletoe.

Clipped mostly from mesquite, the mistletoe is delivered by truck and limousine, by jeep and jalopy to centrally located sheds. In the sheds, open from daylight to 10 P.M., workers, hired for the season, weigh, pack, and ship the mistletoe crop.

The oldest supply company of Texas mistletoe is at Bellaire, a few miles southwest of Houston. The mistletoe, also from mesquite, is picked by farm and ranch families on their own acres, or on the land of neighbors. The crop is delivered to sheds, or packing houses, rented for the season by the supplier.

The company annually handles 30,000 pounds of mistletoes. Sales are made to mail-order customers and to wholesale florists in many sections of the United States.

6

⁂

Myths of Mistletoe

Centuries ago bards sang about mistletoe and mentioned it in their poetry. The plant was famous in ancient folklore of countries as far separated as Iceland and Greece.

No myth of mistletoe is more famous than the one with Balder as its central character. Son of the Norse god Odin, leader in Asgard, Balder was gentle, wise, and handsome. He was beloved by gods of the realm.

The community of the gods was reached by a rainbow bridge, curved and colorful. Of all dwellings in Asgard, the most beautiful was the palace Valhalla.

There came a time when Balder, night after night, wakened from nightmares about his own death. He told his frequent bad dreams to his mother Frigg. She was the goddess for whom Friday, sixth day of our week, is named.

Frigg was determined to protect her son from death. She asked many things in her realm to promise never to harm Balder. A solemn oath was given by animals and birds; by insects, snakes, and other crawling creatures; by fire, water, trees, and metals from the ground, and by every kind of sickness and poison.

To test the promises, the gods of Asgard tried to injure Balder, but could not. They pounded him with fists, cast large rocks at him, and hacked at him with sharp blades. Balder was not bruised, cut, or in any way hurt.

It made the gods happy to know they could not make Balder suffer because he was much loved.

Only one god wanted Balder to die. That one was Loki, god of evil. In disguise, Loki approached Frigg and questioned her about the oath. He wanted to know whether everything in Asgard had sworn to her.

She said only one thing had not. It was mistletoe, a new plant, growing far off. Frigg thought mistletoe was much too young to be asked to make a promise.

Loki was pleased. He traveled to the distant place, found the young plant, and plucked a spray from it.

The evil god carried the mistletoe back to where the others, with respect, still tested Balder.

Loki went up to the blind goddess Hother, twin sister of Balder. The wicked god whispered to her, asking why she did not honor her brother like the other deities.

Hother sadly said she had nothing with which to try to hurt Balder, and besides, she could not see him.

Taking her by the hand, Loki led Hother close to her brother. The god of evil gave the piece of mistletoe to the blind goddess and directed her aim toward her twin. The dartlike twig she threw pierced the body of the young god Balder and killed him.

There are many ancient versions of the myth of Balder. In an Icelandic legend, the death of Balder was by sword. The sword, it was told, was named *mistilteinn*, the word for the plant combined with the word for twig.

In another tale, Balder returned to life after the shaft of mistle-

Hother and Balder

toe was pulled out of his body. The shaft, or dart, was given to his mother Frigg. She was then made secretary of love in the cabinet of the gods. Ever after, in legend mistletoe represented resurrection, life and love.

Druids, pre-Christian priests of Gaul and Celtic Great Britain, associated the oak tree, sacred to them, with the mistletoe growing on it. In their pagan religion, both tree and parasite were important.

Eerie tales described woodland settings for Druid rites held

41

on the sixth night of the new moon. In a grove of oaks, Druid priests in white robes placed a cloth, also pure white, under the tree with the heaviest growth of mistletoe.

A gold implement was chosen by the priests to cut mistletoe from high branches of the oak. The cuttings fell onto the white cloth purposely placed to keep the mistletoe off the ground. It was forbidden that the parasite be allowed to touch the earth in which it did not grow.

The mistletoe, cut down with a gold sickle, or with a sharp gold hook, was placed on a temporary altar constructed of straw. In front of the altar, two pure white bulls were sacrificed to the gods of the pagan priests. Blood flowing from the bulls was bright red. The dramatic contrast of white with red created an uncanny atmosphere to the nighttime scene.

The ceremony of sacrifice was for good fortune at that time and for the future.

Priests were honored and blessed by gifts of mistletoe from the altar. Small pieces of mistletoe, cut to size with a gold blade, were sold to people who could afford to pay. Those worshippers wore their mistletoe charms for good luck and for protection from fiends, witches, and similar evil spirits.

According to ancient accounts, Druid priests, during the ceremonies, embraced and kissed each other. If so, they may have originated the custom of kissing under mistletoe.

An oath asked for by Jesus Christ appears in an ancient Hebrew biography of Jesus of Nazareth. Jesus, it was written, asked all trees to promise not ever to harm him in any way.

Every tree but the mistletoe made the solemn oath to Jesus.

In a grove of oaks, Druid priests in white robes placed a cloth under the tree with the heaviest growth of mistletoe.

Trunks of the trees split down the middle and splintered into small pieces. Limbs and branches also fell apart.

The mistletoe, a tree with roots in the earth at that time, did not split or break up like other trees. It was the only healthy, strong tree standing near Jerusalem, in ancient Palestine, at the time of the crucifixion of Jesus Christ. Mistletoe was cut into boards which were put together for the cross.

After that, according to the Hebrew biography, mistletoe was cursed and its growth stunted. The tree became a parasite plant.

Christians of later centuries forgot the curse. They made religious objects from the parasite mistletoe. Rosaries were carved from wood of the slender stems. The stems also were used to fashion small crosses.

In monasteries, mistletoe leaves were steeped in hot water to make a drink like tea. And monks chewed chips of the wood identified with Jesus.

So-called palm bushes were distributed at Palm Sunday services in the Bavaria of more modern times. Mistletoe for the palm bushes was traditionally cut from willow trees.

The myth of the mistletoe cross was popular in the reign of George I, king of Great Britain and Ireland (1714–1727). In the British Isles, mistletoe was then commonly called Holy Cross wood.

7

❦❦❦❦❦

Superstitions about Mistletoe

"No mistletoe, no luck" was a saying originated long ago by superstitious farmers in Wales. They believed corn crops of their fields would be good whenever mistletoe was plentiful in surrounding woodlands.

The Ainu, aborigines of Japan, worshiped mistletoe. Descendants of the primitive Ainu tribes today cut up leaves of mistletoe and mix small pieces with garden seeds. Seeds combined with the magic mistletoe leaves are supposed to produce great quantities of flowers and vegetables. The Ainu use mistletoe cut from willow trees, sacred in Japan.

A mistletoe superstition in Africa was exactly the opposite of the legend of Balder who was pierced by a mistletoe dart. Warriors of the Walos tribe carried mistletoe to keep from being wounded in battle. Or they put leaves of *tob*, mistletoe in their language, on their bodies as defense against enemies.

Superstitions about protection from bodily harm are fewer in the lore of mistletoe than superstitions concerned with evil spirits and luck, good and bad.

Good luck, according to various superstitions, depends on

45

how and when mistletoe is cut.

For many centuries, mistletoe in Switzerland was shot from trees by arrows. Like ancient Druid priests, the Swiss thought it was bad luck to let mistletoe be in contact with the earth in which it did not grow. But, instead of spreading a cloth to catch falling twigs, the Swiss had to be quick to grab them. And, for good luck, the catch always had to be made with the left hand, never with the right.

In other parts of Europe it is supposed to be bad luck to cut mistletoe. The parasite is knocked off trees with big sticks or with handles of garden tools. Or, it is shot off trees with pistols or rifles. No matter what the method, the mistletoe, for good luck, is caught as it falls, before it hits the earth.

Mistletoe is shot from trees on Maryland's Eastern Shore, part of the Delmarva Peninsula between the Atlantic Ocean and the Chesapeake Bay. The shooting, a matter of convenience, has nothing to do with good luck.

Many Eastern Shore trees, infected by the parasite, are very tall and badly damaged. Even from the tops of extension ladders, it is impossible to reach the mistletoe growth.

Climbing those Eastern Shore trees with their brittle limbs and branches can be dangerous. A thudding fall would surely be bad luck for a person who attempted the climb.

In order to harvest their large crops of mistletoe, farmers on the Shore ask for the cooperation of hunters. The duck season opens at the time when mistletoe should be cut. As a favor or for a fee, duck hunters shoot down the mistletoe which the farmers sell to wholesale florists for holiday decorations.

The Druids' custom of cutting mistletoe at a certain moon phase has come down through the years, but with changes. The times for cutting are dependent today on the summer and winter solstices.

Elsewhere in Europe, mistletoe sprays are fastened above entrance doors to make sure only happiness enters.

The summer solstice is June 22 when the sun is at its northernmost position from the earth's equator. On December 22, the winter solstice, the sun is closest to the equator. Those days are respectively the longest and shortest of the year.

In Scandinavia and other northern countries, mistletoe is harvested on Midsummer Eve, the day before the solstice. In southern climates mistletoe may not yet have berries at the time

47

of the summer solstice. There, picking has to be done when berries are fully formed, or in the period before the winter solstice.

Mistletoe, whenever or wherever harvested, is more important as a symbol of superstitions than as a holiday decoration.

In England, mistletoe used to be worn as a good luck charm. It was also placed over front doors for good luck throughout the year. A similar symbol of good luck is a horseshoe nailed over a barn door.

Elsewhere in Europe, mistletoe sprays are fastened above entrance doors to make sure only happiness enters. And sprigs of mistletoe are placed in rooms to scare off witches.

Farmers in Wales and in rural Worcestershire, a county of England, feed their holiday mistletoe to the cow giving birth to the first calf of the New Year. That, it is claimed, assures good health to the entire dairy herd for the next twelve months.

It is bad luck in Worcestershire to take fresh-cut mistletoe into a home before Christmas Eve. On that day, December 24, it is good luck to throw out the one piece of dried mistletoe kept since the previous Christmas.

In western countries, most holiday superstitions about mistletoe have to do with kissing.

Who is to know where the custom of kissing under mistletoe originated. Was it during pagan ceremonies of the Druids? Or, at festivals in ancient Greece? Or, in the merrymaking of ancient Rome's Saturnalia, festival of Saturn, held in December?

There are many variations of every superstition about mistletoes and kissing. A list of them could number in the hundreds.

Once there was a custom of the kissing-bunch from which a berry was pulled for each kiss. When there was not one more berry on the green-leafed spray, the kissing had to stop. That was the rule, and no cheating was allowed.

It was said a girl not kissed under holiday mistletoe would not be married before the next Christmas.

In certain parts of England, every sprig of mistletoe, hung high as holiday decoration, is burned on Twelfth Night, January 6. If that is not done, unmarried young people who kissed under the mistletoe will never in their lives be bride or groom. They will never marry.

A kissing ball hung from a door lintel or suspended from a center light in a hall is a modern substitute for the kissing-bunch.

Making a kissing ball is not difficult. You need a good supply of mistletoe twigs covered with lots of shiny green leaves and plump white berries. You also have to have patience, time, and a base.

How many twigs you need depends on what you intend to use for the base. It can be a large round ball of styrofoam, or a potato about the size and shape of a baseball. The potato is the better choice because, being about 78 percent water, it will keep the mistletoe moist and fresh through the holidays.

An apple is the right shape for a kissing ball, but it is likely to be too juicy and runny. Its sticky, sweet liquid might drip down on the faces of those kissing under the mistletoe ball.

Spread twigs of mistletoe on old newspapers covering your work surface, a table or kitchen counter. If the stems of the plant are blunt, sharpen them with a paring knife.

Stick the sharp stems into the styrofoam ball, or into the potato. At the circumference of the sphere leave a line like the earth's equator. The space around the middle should measure about one-half inch and not more than three-quarters of an inch.

Place twigs as close together as possible to make a bushy and attractive form. When finished the green-and-white ball should be much larger than the base.

Fit red satin or red velvet ribbon around the circumference.

49

The ribbon or velvet should be exactly the width of the line, one-half inch or three-quarters of an inch. Be sure the ribbon is tight and not likely to slip or sag.

Where the ribbon meets, tie a firm knot, leaving long ends. The ends should measure about ten inches. Make a loop of the ends so the ball can be hung on a hook under the lintel or the hall light.

After the kissing ball is in place, you can hide the hook with one big red bow, or with a circle of tiny red bows, or with any decoration you fancy.

Making a kissing ball is not difficult.

51

8

Medicine from Mistletoe

Medical writers of ancient times mentioned mistletoe as a remedy for diseases of mind and body: Mental illness. Heart ailments. Tumors. And swollen and reddened tongues.

The mystery of mistletoe medicine of the past is how liquid and powdered preparations prescribed for patients were safely made. By what means was the poison removed from mistletoe berries? Were some kinds of medicine made from leaves of the parasite?

Druids gave mistletoe powder to people suffering with heart disease and with palsy, a shaking disease, mostly of old age. No matter what the patient had, medication was prescribed for forty consecutive days.

But the Druids seem to have had little faith in mistletoe as medicine. The pagan priests claimed a sprig of fresh mistletoe worn on a cord or a chain around the neck would cure a patient faster than a mistletoe powder.

> *Medical writers of ancient times mentioned*
> *mistletoe as a remedy for diseases.*

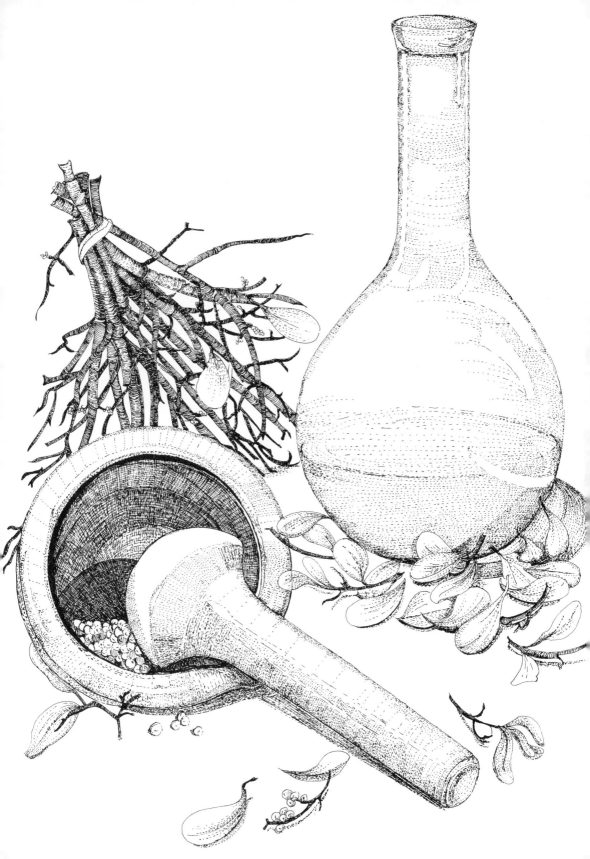

Pliny the Elder, a Roman naturalist, wrote that chewing mistletoe would cure an open sore on the body. Did he mean chew a leaf? Pliny also suggested covering the sore with mistletoe.

Over the centuries, the uses of mistletoe medicines varied with countries of the world.

In Switzerland, all diseases of childhood were supposedly cured by remedies made from the parasite.

The Ainu, aborigines of Japan, made concoctions for treatment of children and grownups. Malay villagers used mistletoe as treatment for women having babies; for snakebite, and for ringworm, a skin disease of people and animals.

Juniper branches with mistletoe attached were brewed like tea by pregnant women of certain Indian tribes in the American Southwest. Twigs of the juniper and its parasite were boiled and treated to make the liquid safe to drink. It relaxed muscles of women when their babies were being born.

Cambodians swallowed a mistletoe medicine to protect themselves from an enemy. Juice from the berries was the main ingredient of the extract the Cambodians took by the dose, like cough syrup.

For three thousand years mistletoe was supposed to cure epilepsy, known in all parts of the world as the falling disease.

Since mistletoe does not fall from the wood it is rooted in, people once thought an epileptic treated with mistletoe would not fall down during a seizure. Mistletoe in either powdered or liquid form was swallowed by the patient. But the epileptic was advised also to wear mistletoe around the neck, or to keep a sprig tucked into clothing.

During the last half of the nineteenth century, mistletoe medicine was considered to be without value. A French biologist flatly stated, in 1869, that the mistletoe family in medicine "offers

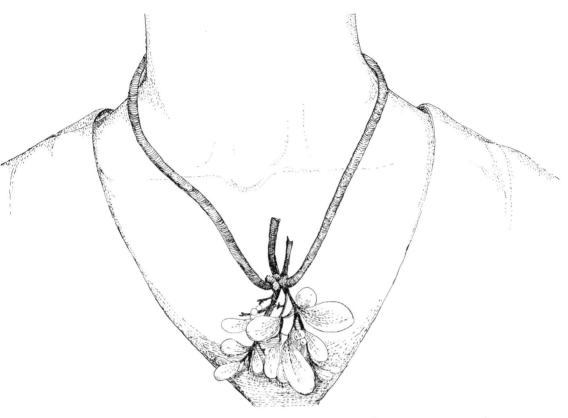

The pagan priests claimed a sprig of fresh mistletoe worn around the neck would cure a patient faster than a mistletoe powder.

us nothing of interest."

After the turn of the twentieth century, mistletoe once again interested certain medical experts. Doctors, chemists, and pharmacologists started to experiment with the parasite in their laboratories.

In 1900 processed mistletoe was the adhesive for a skin plaster like the strip bandages now used for minor cuts. The skin plaster, made in Germany, was not commercially successful. It worked all right, but customers did not like the bad smell and the ugly yellow-green color of the adhesive.

Research with mistletoe medicines increased in the twentieth century.

V. Album was the basis for treatments of illnesses related to the heart, veins, and arteries. That particular mistletoe was also effective in the treatment of one kind of arthritis, and of certain diseases of the nerves.

Extracts of juices from pressed berries of *V. album* have been used in experimental cancer research. Anticancer products were developed in Russia, Switzerland, and in West Germany where extensive research continues.

In the United States, from the late 1950s until 1966, cancer therapy research with *V. album* extract was done at the Roswell Park Memorial Institute, Buffalo, New York. Dr. Oleg Selawry experimented there with "growth inhibitors of plant origin."

V. album extract was the major material of plant origin for the study. The purpose was to find ways to inhibit, that is to decrease and prevent, the growth of cancer tumors.

Mistletoe, official flower of the state of Oklahoma, became a cancer research plant there because of a professor's curiosity.

Dr. Alfred J. Weinheimer was already well-known for his drug research when, in 1971, he first collected mistletoe to study. As professor of chemistry at the University of Oklahoma at Norman, he was a specialist in preparing extracts from marine organisms. These extracts were for drug tests.

The research, part of the University's program of marine chemistry and pharmacology, was done with organisms collected in the Caribbean Sea.

On a December day in 1971, Professor Weinheimer went on a mistletoe hunt around Norman with his children. The family intended to pick mistletoe for decorating their home, and as holiday gifts for friends and neighbors.

Dr. Weinheimer became suddenly curious about whether

mistletoe did have cancer curing properties. He knew about modern medical experiments with the parasite and, also, had read ancient folklore about mistletoe medicine.

For his studies, he needed lots of mistletoe. Picking it was no problem because there were six Weinheimer children to help. With a working crew of that size it was easy to gather enough mistletoe for his laboratory.

Extracts from the berries were sent to the National Cancer Institute of the National Institutes of Health. Tests showed the presence of an agent, or compound, in mistletoe that one day might be useful in cancer treatment.

There was much more research to be done before a drug could be developed. And more research meant that a greater number of mistletoe berries had to be collected.

In 1972, 125 gallons of mistletoe berries were harvested from clumps of mistletoe picked within a 50-mile radius of Norman. The volunteer collectors were mostly Boy Scouts from several troops.

Boy Scouts again collected for the lab in 1973. But Dr. Weinheimer had to have many more volunteers. He needed people to collect the mistletoe, to pick berries from the stems, and to help with freezing. Freezing of the berries had to be done within a day or no more than two days after the picking.

Like superstitious people, Dr. Weinheimer insisted that the mistletoe must not touch the earth. But his reason was practical. If clumps of mistletoe hit the ground with a thud, valuable berries might be smashed.

Dr. Weinheimer's instruction to volunteers included a warning against eating berries. It was important for every volunteer, child or adult, to understand the "berries are toxic if eaten."

Raw berries are poisonous to people. No one yet knows whether extracted juices from mistletoe berries will at some future time be a sure cure for cancer.

9

❦❦❦❦❦

Questions and Some Answers

Mistletoes are full of surprises. Even scientists who study the parasites are sometimes astonished by what they observe: A mistletoe species suddenly growing on a new host. A kind of tree beginning to reject a type of mistletoe it once accepted.

The unpredictable events intrigue botanists, forest pathologists, and other specialists concerned with the growth and control of mistletoes. They are subjects of countless and continuing research projects, and, yet, questions about them keep cropping up.

How many more years will it take to find answers to what scientists are asking about the mistletoes? In whatever century today's questions are answered, later questions will undoubtedly puzzle experts.

Will a healthy growth of mistletoe ever increase the life of a host? Perhaps a weakened host might take back some nutrients, moisture, and minerals stolen from it by a certain type of mistletoe.

V. *album* sneaked into the United States by having its roots concealed in a host never identified. Could *Viscum cruciatum*

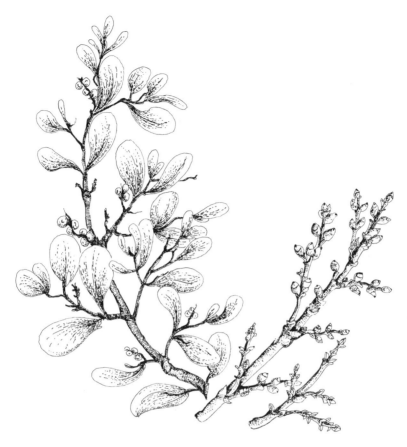

Leafy mistletoe (left) *and dwarf mistletoe* (right) *together*

immigrate the same way? *V. cruciatum*, chiefly parasitic on olive trees in Mediterranean countries of Europe, would add interest to American mistletoe crops: its berries are red.

Why should just one species of leafy mistletoe have red berries instead of white? Or *is* it the only one? Who is to know whether another red-berried leafy mistletoe will some day be discovered?

The big question unlikely ever to be satisfactorily answered is: What is the origin of the word mistletoe? Dictionaries do not

59

agree, nor do mistletoe experts.

One choice from English is the old word *mistion*, for mingled, combined with *tod* meaning bushy mass. Species of the parasite joined to, or mingled with, the host often do become bushy masses.

But what if the first part of mistletoe comes from *mixen*, the Anglo-Saxon word for dung? That would be sensible. Dung has several meanings; one is bird droppings. And, as you know, seeds of most kinds of mistletoe are planted by bird droppings.

Another Anglo-Saxon word, *mistl-tan*, means a different twig. And mistletoe twigs are certainly different, unlike any others.

It is a challenge to look up the word in several sources. See for yourself the choices of origin. Can you decide from what language mistletoe comes?

Whatever is unknown about the mistletoes, one thing is certain: their family is one of the most interesting in nature, and in history from earliest times.

Index

61

The Author

GRAY JOHNSON POOLE was first published at age thirteen. She has since written for newspapers, industry, magazines, and book publishers. Many of her books were done in collaboration with her late husband, Lynn Poole. Dodd, Mead has published more than a dozen Poole titles, including *Nuts from Forest, Orchard, and Field* (Gray Johnson Poole, 1974).

Mrs. Poole, a former resident of Baltimore, now makes her home in Los Angeles.